To the real Frances Anne

With thanks to Nancy Van Laan
and to Sensei William Johns of the William Johns Karate Academy

Copyright © 2003 by Mary Leary
All rights reserved
Distributed in Canada by Douglas & McIntyre Ltd.
Color separations by Chroma Graphics PTE Ltd.
Printed and bound in the United States of America by Berryville Graphics
Designed by Nancy Goldenberg
First edition, 2003
10 9 8 7 6 5 4 3 2 1

Library of Congress Cataloging-in-Publication Data
Leary, Mary.
    Karate girl / Mary Leary.— 1st ed.
        p.   cm.
    Summary: Hoping to protect her younger brother from school bullies, a girl
begins taking karate classes.
    ISBN 0-374-33977-5
    [1. Karate—Fiction.   2. Brothers and sisters—Fiction.]   I. Title.

PZ7.L46367 Kar 2003
[E]—dc21
                                                        2002035420

Karate Girl

Mary Leary

Farrar Straus Giroux / New York

My brother, Eli, can be a pain sometimes, but I am patient with him. I know he admires me.

One day last spring, some mean kids started bugging Eli and made him cry. I was angry but scared and didn't know what to do.

The next day, I talked to my best friend, June.
"Come to karate class with me tomorrow," she said.
June had started taking karate a while ago. She'd
been trying to get me to come to class for a long time.

That night, I could not sleep.

I kept thinking about how I would use karate to get back at the bullies.

Before class, June introduced me to her teacher, the sensei.

He asked why I was interested in karate. I told him about the mean kids.

"Karate is not only about self-defense," the sensei said. "It teaches us to have self-control and confidence. To be sure enough of oneself to avoid a fight—that is what karate is about. It takes a long time to learn and much dedication."

I felt ready to learn, so I signed up.

Class was held at a place called a dojo, in a big room with a mat. Everybody was wearing a white robe called a gi, with a belt around the waist. June told me that the color of the belt shows what level you've reached. It is based on ability, not on how big or how old you are.

White is for beginners, like me. Black is for someone very accomplished, like the sensei. There are many colors in between: yellow, red, blue, green, and brown. To move through all the different levels takes years of practice and many classes.

I went to class twice a week. At the beginning of class, the sensei had us do our breathing and relaxation exercises. We closed our eyes and thought only about our breathing. At first it was hard and my mind would wander, but after a few lessons it became easier. My thoughts would quiet down and I could focus on one thing with all my attention.

After breathing and relaxation, we did warm-ups to get us loose and ready to move. Then we could practice our moves with focus and proper position.

The sensei taught us different kinds of blocks, punches, kicks, and stances. We would practice each one over and over again until we were sure and quick.

Then we put them together in different combinations. Each combination is called a kata.

After you practice the moves together for a long time, they become automatic. The kata seems like a beautiful dance done with an invisible partner.

But the kata is really a series of self-defense moves, and the invisible partner would be your opponent.

This kata has a blocking and a kicking stance. It was the first kata I learned.

I got better and better at karate. I learned my concentration is best when I am alone and it is quiet. The sensei says karate is not to be used to show off.

After practicing a kata all summer, I performed it and was promoted to a yellow belt.

In addition to knowing the moves, I had learned how to focus and concentrate. This gave me the kind of confidence that comes with really knowing something.

When school started in the fall, the mean kids tried to pick on Eli again. But I was ready.

I stood up to them and showed them I was not afraid.

"My sister knows karate," Eli told them.

"So what?" they said.

"So that means if I absolutely have to fight, I can and will," I said.

"Karate girl!" they called me, and walked away.

I smiled. I liked being a karate girl.

I still do karate. My brother is taking lessons, too.

In karate there is a saying—when you bow to the universe, the universe bows back.